OH, NO! Granny Lost Her Hearing Aid in Africa!

Dear Amani + Malaika,
Have fun reading this funny story! ☺

Author Mindy Sawyer

♡ *Mindy Sawyer*

© Copyright June 2019

Mindy Sawyer Enterprises

You can email the author, Mindy Sawyer at WRITERGAL9825@yahoo.com

Website: https://funnyeducationalbooks.com

This book is dedicated to my son, Larry.
You are an amazing miracle and
I'll love you forever.

Granny smiled and said, "Okay, everyone we are ready for our African adventure with our expert guide, Dayo!"

Dayo gave them a big smile. "Welcome everyone! Yes, my name is Dayo, and in my native Nigerian language Dayo means 'joy is here', so, let's all have some fun!"

Nine-year-old Mikey shouted, "Granny, I'm so excited! I've been researching African animals and I saved information about them on my computer tablet!"

Granny smiled. "That's brilliant, Mikey! Becca, are you ready to go?"

Without looking-up from her cell phone Becca muttered, "Um, sure Gram."

"Alrighty my dears." said Granny. "I've got my trusty old camera and we are ready for our African safari adventure!"

Granny said, "OH, NO! That cute little monkey just grabbed my hearing aid! Oh, well, I'm sure I'll be fine without it."

Mikey said, "That cute monkey is a chimpanzee, Granny. My tablet says that chimps are close relatives to humans."

Dayo said, "That's right, Mikey. Like humans, chimps can walk upright, they hug to show affection, and they can use tools! They can use rocks as tools to open nuts, and sticks as tools to remove and eat insects from nests."

Mikey shouted, **"GRANNY, ROCK PYTHON SNAKE!"**

Granny said, "No thank you dear – I don't want to talk like a snake,' but, I must get a picture of that adorable monkey and friendly snake! How sweet - the snake is giving the monkey a big hug!"

Mikey pointed at the snake and shouted, "No, I didn't say 'Granny talk like a snake', I said, 'Granny **ROCK PYTHON SNAKE!**'"

4

Granny said sadly, "Oh, no! My camera's flash scared away the big, friendly snake and the cute little monkey!"

"Granny," said Mikey, "it's a good thing your camera flash scared the snake away because it was NOT giving the monkey a hug. The Rock Python snake is a constrictor that can crush and swallow its prey."

"Oh, my! That poor little monkey was almost HISS-tory!" winked Granny.

Mikey laughed, "You're talking like a snake after all Granny!"

FLASH!

"Okay everyone, after all that excitement it's time to get in the tour vehicle for our safari," said Dayo.

Mikey pointed, "Granny, look at the wildebeest!"

Granny said, "I beg your pardon, Mikey. I may not look my best right now, but I do NOT look like a hideous beast."

Mikey laughed, "No, I didn't say 'Granny, looks like a hideous beast', I said 'Granny, look at the wildebeest!' This trip is going to be very interesting without your hearing aid, Granny."

Dayo said, "A herd of zebras is also called a dazzle. They have super powerful kicks for protection from lions and other predators."

"That reminds me of a joke," said Mikey. "Do you know why zebras hate coloring books?"

Granny said, "No, why do zebras hate coloring books?"

Mikey answered, "Because they don't like to stay between the LIONS."

Becca laughed. "Okay, I've got one! What does a zebra call his best friend?"

"What?" Mikey asked.

Becca answered, "His Zee-Bro."

"Elephants are the biggest, heaviest animal on land," said Mikey.

"That's right, Mikey," agreed Dayo. "A male elephant can weigh over 13,000 pounds. Elephants cannot jump, but they can swim. If they are in deep water, they can stick their trunk up out of the water and use it like a snorkel to breathe air. Elephants can also use their trunks for eating, drinking, spraying water for a bath, and to hug and caress each other. A baby elephant will even suck its trunk, like a human baby sucks its thumb."

"Oh, no!" said Mikey. "Those spotted hyenas are hiding in the grass. Are they going to attack the baby elephant? I thought hyenas were scavengers."

Dayo looked concerned. "Hyenas are scavengers that eat animals that are not alive, but they are also skilled hunters. Elephants are endangered, so I'm worried about that baby elephant."

"Wow!" exclaimed Mikey. "That bull elephant chased the hyenas away! It's a good thing the bull elephant was alert."

"Yes, it's a good thing the bull elephant was not sleeping, because then he'd be a bull-dozer!" laughed Granny.

Mikey said, "Look at the giant ostriches!"

"Yes," said Dayo. "Besides being the largest bird in the world, it has the largest egg in the world. One ostrich egg is equal to 24 chicken eggs! It also has the largest eyes of any land animal."

Mikey said, "That's amazing! My tablet says that some ostriches can get the bird flu, and the bird flu can sometimes make people sick."

Granny chuckled, "Oh, don't worry about the bird flu, Mikey - I hear its TWEETABLE!"

Dayo said, "The giraffe is the tallest animal in the world and eats acacia leaves from the tops of tall trees."

Mikey said, "The baby giraffe is so cute and amazing. I read it can stand and walk within an hour of being born!"

Dayo said, "That's right Mikey. When born the baby giraffe drops 6 feet to the ground. It needs to stand up quickly so it can drink milk from its mother. Uh, oh. I see two female lions crawling in the grass toward the baby giraffe! I'm worried because female lions are fierce hunters in a pride

"WOW!" Cried Mikey. "The mother giraffe kicked the lion away from her baby!"

"If I wasn't impressed, I'd be **LION**," chuckled Granny.

Dayo laughed. "The giraffe's kick is very powerful. The ostrich we saw also has a powerful kick. The giraffe and the ostrich both have a kick that is so powerful it can sometimes kill a lion. However, it looks like those two lions will be okay."

Mikey shouted, "Granny, rhino! Rhino!"

Granny looked surprised. "Mikey, dear, I'm not a wino. I only drink a little wine now and then."

Mikey smiled. "No, Granny, I didn't say 'Granny, wino,' I said 'Granny, RHINO!'"

Dayo laughed. "The rhino's horn is made of keratin – just like your hair and nails. A group of rhinos is called a crash."

Mikey said, "My tablet says the water buffalo have the longest horns of any animal.

Dayo said, "That's right, Mikey. Their horns can reach 13 feet across, and they use them for protection. The hippos are interesting too. Hippos are the second heaviest land animal, and one hippo can weigh as much as three small cars!"

Mikey smiled, "What do you call a hippo covered in mud?"

"What?" asked Becca.

Mikey replied, "A hippopota-MESS!"

Mikey said, "Look at the beautiful impala antelope. It's easy for me to remember the impala's name, because the markings on their tail end remind me of the letter 'M' for impala."

Dayo said, "'That's clever, Mikey. However, these impalas may be in danger. Do you see the leopard in the sausage tree? It looks like it's ready to jump!"

Mikey yelled, "Run, impala, run!!!"

"Whew!" said Mikey. "Looks like the impala made it!"

"Yes," agreed Dayo. "Although the predators we've seen are fierce hunters, most of their efforts will fail. In one study of leopards hunting during the day, only 3 out of 64 attempts at catching prey were successful."

Mikey shouted, "Look! Kudu! Kudu!"

"Who do?" asked Granny.

"Voo-doo?" asked Becca.

"You do?" joked Dayo.

Mikey laughed. "No! Kudu! It's an African antelope with awesome, curvy horns!"

Dayo said, "Yes, Mikey. The Kudu male is famous for its big, curvy horns. However, one of the strangest events in Africa relates to the kudu's dung. Once a year in South Africa there is a kudu dung-spitting contest."

Becca looked up from her phone. "Ewww, gross! Kudu dung spitting? I'll stick to spitting watermelon seeds."

"Wow, cool! Look at the pangolins!" said Mikey.

Dayo added, "Yes, that is a giant pangolin. As you can see, she carries her baby on her back. The protective plates on her back are made of keratin, like your hair and nails. When frightened the pangolin can curl up into a tight ball."

Mikey said, "My tablet says that the entire wild dog pack helps protect and care for the cubs."

Dayo said, "Yes, Mikey. African wild dogs work together to care for the young, and they also work together when hunting. When eating they share the food with the whole group - even those that are too young, or too old, to hunt."

Mikey yelled, "Wow! Look at that cheetah go!"

Dayo laughed. "Yes, Mikey. You may have heard that the Cheetah is the fastest land animal. It can run 60-75 miles per hour. It's chasing an African Hare."

Mikey said, "The hare made it safely into its hole in the ground!"

Granny said, "Hey, Mikey, do you know why a cheetah can never play hide and seek?"

"No, why Granny?"

"Because he's always SPOTTED."

Dayo said, "I've arranged for a delightful surprise. You can all meet a special friend of mine. We will drive to his village now."

When they arrived at the village, an African man who was holding a bird approached Dayo and spoke in an African language. Dayo then said, "This man is my friend, Masamba. He is a Yao Tribesman, and the bird he is holding is a honeyguide bird. Masamba invited us to join him in following the honeyguide bird. It may lead us to honey in a bee's hive."

"Wow! That would be awesome!" Mikey exclaimed.

Masamba and the honeyguide bird made bird sounds to each other. The group followed the bird as it flew from tree to tree.

Dayo explained, "The honeyguide bird has helped Yao Tribesmen and other African tribes find honey for hundreds of years."

Soon the group stopped by a tree where there were bees buzzing about. Masamba set fire to a bundle of leaves and held it near the hive.

Dayo said, "The smoke from the bundle of burning leaves calms the bees so that Masamba can get the honey out of the hive. He will give some of the leftover beeswax to the hungry bird. He'll leave some of the wax in the tree so the bees can rebuild and make more honey. It's important not to kill a bee or the other bees might attack."

"Oh, I'm not worried," said Granny. "I'll just tell the bees to BUZZ-off!!" Mikey laughed. "Yes, Granny, or I could protect us with a BUZZ-ooka!" Becca smiled. "Or, you could ask the bees to mind their own BUZZ-ness."

"Yum!" said Mikey. "This honeycomb is delicious! Thanks so much, Masamba!"

'Yes, thanks!" said Becca.

"Delicious! Thank you!" said Granny. "Look! There is a bee on my honeycomb. Since I'm holding a bee, I guess my eyes are beautiful, because beauty is in the eyes of the BEE-holder!"

Dayo laughed. "Okay, if you're not too BUZZY, it's time to continue our safari.

After arriving, the group followed Dayo and walked to a lovely lake and waterfall.

Suddenly Mikey shouted, "GRANNY! GOLIATH FROG!"

"No, thanks, Mikey. I don't want to go lie with a dog." said Granny.

Mikey laughed. "No, I didn't say 'Granny, go lie with a dog.' I said, 'Granny, Goliath Frog'. The Goliath Frog is the biggest, most awesome frog in the world!"

Dayo nodded her head. "That's right Mikey. The Goliath Frog is the biggest frog in the world! It can weigh over 7 pounds and jump over 10 feet!

Mikey yelled, "OH, NO! A crocodile is going to eat the Goliath Frog!"

"Granny, your camera's flash scared away the Nile Crocodile!" Said Mikey.

Dayo looked relieved. "Granny, I'm very happy that your camera's flash scared away the crocodile, because the Goliath Frog is in danger of becoming extinct."

Mikey smiled. "Good job, Granny!"

Granny smiled and said, "Dayo, your name means joy and you've certainly brought joy to all of us! Besides being a fun and wonderful guide, we feel like we've made a new friend."

Dayo agrees, "Yes, this has been fun for me, too, and your funny jokes made me laugh. And the best part is that I have met all of you!"

Becca smiled, "Group hug and selfie time!"

More books by Mindy Sawyer available on Amazon.com!

OH, NO! Granny Lost Her Hearing Aid in the Amazon!
is the first book in this series, and is just as hilarious as the rest! While visiting the rainforest in South America with her two grandchildren Granny's hearing aid falls into the river. Fun and excitement ensue as everyone learns about some interesting, (and some dangerous) Amazon rainforest animals!

A–Z Amazing Animals of the Amazon Rainforest of South America by Mindy Sawyer
is a fascinating book that is educational and FUN for all ages, and it can help children learn to read! Read about real Amazon animals such as a lizard that has a third eye, and a bird that smells like manure! Learn fun and interesting facts about the world's heaviest snake, largest rodent, loudest land animal, and a fish that can bark! These and many more amazing animals live in the Amazon Rainforest and are in this book!

FUN FOR ALL AGES:
1.Older children will have fun learning unusual facts about animals.
2. Children who are beginning readers can enjoy taking turns reading with an adult, as this is a K-2 "We Can Both Read" book!
3.Younger children can enjoy the vibrant photos and learn the animal names as an adult reads with them

Gabby Meets Vlad the Vampire by Mindy Sawyer
is a hilarious story that also has important safety tips for children. Vlad the Vampire tries to trick a little girl named Gabby, but she has some tricks up her sleeve! It's a funny story with a surprise ending. (Plus, it's a lot of fun to read with a vampire accent!)

40045970R00027

Made in the USA
San Bernardino, CA
23 June 2019